THREE DATES
WITH YOU

A FLIRTY NOVELLA

LAUREN BLAKELY

LAUREN BLAKELY BOOKS

ALSO BY LAUREN BLAKELY

Wanderlust

Part-Time Lover

One Love Series

The Sexy One

The Only One

The Hot One

The Knocked Up Plan

Come As You Are

Sports Romance

Most Valuable Playboy

Most Likely to Score

Standalones

Stud Finder

The V Card

The Real Deal

Unbreak My Heart

The Break-Up Album

The Caught Up in Love Series

The Pretending Plot (previously
called *Pretending He's Mine*)

ABOUT

A flirty friends-to-lovers novella starring a tough but feisty heroine and a hero who's determined to prove he's worth a shot...

In theory, dating again sounds easy. In practice, it's terrifying. Especially if the guy you want to take a chance with is your good friend. But as we gallivant around London, Sam makes his case for taking a chance on three dates with him.

Gulp. Here I go...

THREE DATES WITH YOU

By Lauren Blakely

Want to be the first to learn of sales, new releases, preorders and special freebies? Sign up for my VIP mailing list here!

1

MAEVE

It's an hour till closing and Trouble has just walked into my bar.

You could set your clock by it—if a customer is going to be a problem, expect it to be one of the last customers of the night.

I eye the tall guy sporting a long ponytail, leaning against my precious jukebox. He runs a finger down the list of song choices, clicks a button, then glances over at me.

Or, more specifically, at my boobs.

I roll my eyes, then grab a dishrag from the shelf behind me to clean the pint glasses while "Pour Some Sugar On Me" blasts over the speakers.

"I think you have an admirer," Cat says as she grabs a clean glass and pours a beer. She's my right hand at the bar along with Billy, my new mixologist. Sure, I still miss Dean, my old business partner at The Magpie—but these two make life here fun.

"He's definitely checking you out," Cat says, tipping her head toward Ponytail. "And he's kinda cute."

Oh, sweet girl. "Tip from one woman to another—stay away from guys like that. Guys like that are trouble."

"What do you mean, trouble?" She tilts her head to the side as she hands the customer his beer then chalks the drink up to his tab.

I raise one hand, count off the list. "One: he's been making eyes at my chest ever since he walked in."

"Well, empirically speaking, your boobs are great." Cat shrugs.

"Even if I had a porn-star worthy rack, my face is up here, and a little eye contact wouldn't go astray." I hold up a second finger. "Reason number two: he's been here five minutes, and he's already asked Billy to send a drink to that woman over there"—I point to a lady in red standing with another woman in one corner of the bar—"and that one there." This time, I point to a woman in a "bride-to-be" sash.

"Ugh." Cat rolls her green eyes.

"Double ugh," I agree. "And reason number three: his pickup line. It's sure to be atrocious."

"How do you know?" she asks.

"Call it a special skill," I say as I place a glass on the rack. "When you've worked the bar for as long as I have, sometimes you just have a feeling when a man has absolutely no game in the pickup line department."

"I've never met a pickup line I've liked," Cat laments, then darts her eyes to the jukebox. "Here he comes. Need me to run interference?"

"It's fine. I've got this," I reply, and Cat moves away to serve another customer as Pony-tail approaches the bar.

I turn to face him, flashing my most professional smile. "What can I get you?"

"I was hoping for something real . . ." His eyes dance to my chest again. ". . . tasty, if you know what I mean."

Aaaand we have a winner, ladies and gents.

Cat hides a smile behind her hand, disguising it with a cough, and I heave a deep breath.

"We have many tasty options here on our menu." I gesture to the folder on the bar. After all, there's no need to be rude. "But if that was a terrible pickup line and you were hoping to perhaps order some of this?" I gesture to my chest. "I am most definitely not for sale."

Ponytail shrugs and taps the bar with a too-long nail. "Your loss, lady."

"Sure it is." I gesture to Billy as he walks closer. "If you'd like to order an actual drink for yourself —not for another one of our patrons—Billy can help you out. If not, he'd be happy to order you a taxi and you can head on home."

Ponytail gapes, a la goldfish.

I don't wait for his reply. Instead, I turn and walk to the other end of the bar to prep the bottles of booze I'll need for an industry trade show tomorrow, adrenaline pumping through me. It's not the first time I've been hit on here, and it won't be the last. Something about being a bartender—I guess people figure I'm easy prey.

Clap. Clap. Clap.

I look up, searching for the slow-clapper.

And there he is.

Sam.

My old business partner's close friend.

And the subject of some of my wildest dreams.

Not that I gave him a second thought until recently. When I first met him a few years ago, Sam was married, which placed him firmly in the "just mates" column.

As Dean's friends, we always found ourselves at the same parties and events. Sam was the incredibly hot, incredibly unavailable guy with the best dirty jokes.

It was just a shame I hadn't seen him much since Dean had moved to the States.

"You handled that well," Sam says, tipping his head toward Ponytail as he lopes out of the bar. "That could have been a challenging situation."

"Thanks." I shrug, like it's no big deal. "This isn't my first rodeo."

"I bet. I'm sure you get hit on a lot."

"I wouldn't say a lot." I make a face. "But enough. I definitely get hit on enough."

"What constitutes 'enough' bar pickups?" he asks, playfulness in his tone. "Is there some kind of national standard?"

"You tell me," I reply, since Sam's a bar owner himself and sometimes he stops by mine. "What's your limit?"

"It's not a question of quantity for me, but rather quality." Sam's dark eyes fix on mine, and is that a hint of flirtation in his sexy American accent?

Heat fizzes inside me. "I feel the same way."

He smiles, and oh, that sexy, crooked smile—it's like champagne, sending tiny frissons of excitement through my body.

"'Scuse me, love? A refill?" someone calls from the other end of the bar.

I hold up one finger to Sam, *be right back*, and head over to grab the gentleman his drink.

As I pour the beer, I covertly check out Sam once again. His dark eyes are on his phone, his gorgeous smile the perfect pair to them, like gin and vermouth.

He runs a hand over that sexy jawline, and my fingers itch, wanting in on a piece of that action too.

What if he stayed until close and we shared a drink? If we talked until late in the night, and then talking led to me touching that jaw? If he leaned in close as he kissed me goodnight, what would he smell like?

How would he taste?

Get a grip, Maeve.

He's just a man.

A recently available man.

Who happens to be incredibly handsome.

But there's a reason I don't date.

I've made too many bad choices. Plenty of guys seem good on paper and then turn out to be total wastes of time.

Take Jeremy, the best and worst of them. Went to Cambridge, nabbed a fancy law degree, dressed like James Bond. He took me to museums and cooked for me. He wrote poetry on the side and would read it to me while we sat on the balcony.

It was perfect. Until I found out Jeremy was doing private poetry readings for some other woman at the same time.

But that's all in the past, because I've found the perfect relationship. I pour my soul into this one, and in return, it just gets better and better. It's a lot of work, but The Magpie will never let me down.

She's *my* bar.

God, I love how that sounds.

And that's why I don't need to focus on what-ifs with men like Sam, even if he makes me smile, and is easy to talk to, and looks like sex on a stick.

I hand the beer to the customer then return to the man in question, who's settled in at a bar stool. "What can I get you? I'd have thought you'd be working."

"I took the night off. I'm at the industry trade show tomorrow and wanted time to get my ducks in a row. Are you going—?"

"Yes," I rush the word almost like he's asked me out, which is ridiculous, because it's a trade show, not dinner and a movie, and he's a mate, not a date.

"Ah, good. I was hoping I could ask you something," he says, and my body wants to say *yes, yes, yes*, even before it knows the question.

It's been a few months since Sam's divorce. Perhaps Sam is feeling these same stirrings of potential between us as I am. Perhaps he's *seeing* me, not as Dean's mate, not as a friend of a friend, but as a woman.

An interested woman.

"Shoot," I reply cool, calm, and collected.

"I'm making a Buck's fizz for an event tomorrow and I'm fresh out of orange for our garnish, and the only stores open this late aren't exactly purveyors of quality produce." He makes an apologetic face. "Do you happen to have any oranges I could borrow?"

Oranges.

He doesn't want to see me.

He wants to see my . . . oranges.

"Sure," I reply evenly.

"Thank you. You are truly a goddess of the bar world," Sam says. "Now I'll have time to dehydrate them overnight. And I'll have more sent to your bar tomorrow as soon as the grocer opens."

"No need." I wave a hand, dismissing the notion. "Our fruit guy often delivers extra."

"So it's fate then. You had some in my time of need." His eyes smolder, that hint of flirtation back again.

But this time, I douse the bubbles of hope in my stomach before they can fully develop. He's not here for me, and that's fine. We're just friends, and that's okay.

Billy, Cat, and I close the bar, and he's one of the last patrons to leave, a bag of oranges slung over his shoulder.

Yes, the last patrons of the night sure are trouble.

Only this time, I didn't see it coming.

2

MAEVE

The next morning, I get ready for the event. I pack my slinky dress into a garment bag, along with my heels, then lace up my trainers, since I'll spend the afternoon setting up a booth.

I swipe on some winged eyeliner, praying it stays set during my setup session. Because I want to look like a professional business owner.

Not for any other reason.

My phone trills with an incoming call, and I put my

makeup away and glance at the screen.

Dean.

Smiling, I accept his call to video chat. He's in his kitchen, looking chipper, and I can practically smell the eggs and mushrooms sizzling in the pan behind him. Omelets, of course.

"What time is it there?" I ask. "Six-something?"

He laughs. "Six-thirty. Fitz has a flight soon, so I thought I'd get up and make him breakfast."

"What a good fiancé you are," I tease. "Though I'd be careful. Isn't an omelet a little ambitious? I seem to remember you burning food at the bar occasionally."

"One time is not 'occasionally,' and you've never let me forget it. I'm an excellent chef. And my cooking makes him very happy."

"I don't think it's the cooking." I laugh.

"It's true. I keep my man satisfied in every way," he says, then sets the phone so I can still see him as he works, sautéing the mushrooms. "Tell me about you. Is there any special someone on the scene?"

I shake my head. "Not exactly."

"Two special someones?" he teases, and I laugh again.

"I'm in a full-time relationship with this amazing bar you and your man gave me," I say, then tone down the teasing for a beat. "Thank you again. I love it to bits."

"I know you do, and I'm glad, but don't be all work and no play, Maeve. If it's meeting someone that's a problem, perhaps you could try Tinder."

"You've been in a relationship too long if you've already

forgotten how dismal the prospects are here," I tease.

"Someday, someone will walk in there, and love will knock *you* on your arse," he says.

I snort. "Even if it does, you of all people know how hard it is to sustain a relationship with the hours we work. Unless I meet someone who also works till two or three in the morning, then sleeps till midday, it's pretty hard."

"Hard, but not impossible." A flicker of seriousness crosses his face. "But is that really all that's holding you back from dating right now?"

No. But I don't want to dampen his mood. "Can we talk about something else please? I know I'll only have you for another few minutes before your lover demands you feed him those scrambled eggs," I tease.

"It's an *omelet*. I can cook an omelet," he corrects in the tone of the long-suffering. "What's on today? Many people booked in at The Magpie?"

"A few," I reply. "But that tasting event's this afternoon, so I'm leaving Billy and Cat to man the fort."

"Ah, yes. Of course it is," he says. "You look amazing, lady. Maybe you'll meet someone there."

I push away the thought of Sam. He's a friend—nothing more, nothing less. "While a fellow bar owner might be the only person I could sustain a relationship with, I doubt I'll meet Mr. Right."

"How about Mr. Right Now?" he asks.

"I don't have the energy for a one-night stand."

"Maeve, all I want is for you to keep an open mind," he says.

"Open mind, closed legs." I snap my fingers. "Sounds like a good slogan. We should put it on a T-shirt. But will you please let my lack-of-love life be?"

He stops moving the spatula to lean closer to the camera. His eyes shine with concern. "I just feel a little guilty for leaving you alone."

"Don't you worry," I say, waving a hand dismissively. "I'm a badass bar owner who can handle herself. But I appreciate you looking out for me. Though . . . I do think something's burning behind you."

A bit of steam comes off the mushrooms.

"Shite, I think you've cursed me," he says with a laugh. "Text me later and tell me how it went?"

"Will do. Bye for now."

I turn off the video and apply my final swipe of mascara. A

quick glance in the mirror to check that my leggings and crop top are still in place, and yep. I'm ready to shift some crates.

Just one more thing. I snap a pic and send it to my friend Sierra. She's a bartender in San Francisco, and a kindred spirit.

Maeve: Do I look ready to rule the world?

Sierra: Leggings are the uniform for world domination, so I'd say yes. Tasting event today?

Maeve: You know me so well!

Sierra: Knock 'em dead, badass babe. And tell me if you meet any sexy Americans. Oh wait, you already met one .

Maeve: Troublemaker!

She's not wrong, but once again, I force thoughts of Sam from my mind.

I grab some face powder for touch-ups and the box of decorations and posters, then head downstairs, where I call a Lyft to jet over to the event hotel. I'm one of the first to arrive, which doesn't surprise me. I've always been punctual. Better to be too early than too late. It settles my nerves, knowing I'll have all the time I need.

At my booth, the courier has delivered. I pull out my glassware from the boxes and set it and my ingredients up first. I work up a sweat, organizing rocks glasses, setting up the ice machine, and shifting the bar back around.

Next, I open my box of decorations and pull out the gold

tassels, my eyes on the booth behind me. I think I'll string them from the top, but the event starts soon—which means I'll need to find a ladder, pronto. I place the tassels down, ready to start my search.

"It's fate."

I spin around, searching for the familiar deep, baritone voice.

Sam stands in the booth next to mine, his dark eyes glinting. "Seems like not only are we both attending today, but our booths are next to each other."

"Why, so they are, makes it more fun."

"Lucky us," he says and he draws me into a hug. He feels so solid pressed against me, and he smells like clean sandalwood. I catch myself breathing him in and step back.

Something about Sam feels like home. We might not have

the whole gang on one conti-
nent anymore, but Sam's still
here, so it's best for me to keep
the naughty thoughts all
locked up

"So tell me—how did the
oranges go?" I ask, looking over
his shoulder at the already set up
booth.

He walks to the bar and
grabs a perfectly candied piece
of fruit. "Would you like to try?"

"No. Thank you," I blurt,
then look away. When did it get
so hot in here?

I need a change in topic, and
I need it fast. "How's Sticks and
Stones doing?" I ask, inquiring
about his bar.

"No complaints. Nice and
busy. That's how we like it,
right? Tourist season's winding
down, but you know that."

"I'll miss them. I love the
tourists and their big American
tips."

"Hey, now, didn't you and Dean always say that they had the worst taste in drinks?"

"That is not true!" I say. "The occasional American will try to order a Long Island iced tea, but I can usually convince them to try our specialty drinks."

"I bet you can be very persuasive," he says, and is that flirtation in his voice?

"I can," I reply, flirting right back, because why the heck not? "If I steer them away from vodka slushies, I figure I am doing them a great service indeed."

Sam shudders. "Just yesterday, I had a guy trying to order a strawberry daiquiri."

"And I trust you refused."

"As one does."

I gesture to his booth. "What drink are you plying the crowds with here? The Buck's Fizz, I presume."

"Since you saved me with the

oranges, yes. Our specialty. And I'm guessing you're doing your old-fashioned? You make magic with that one, Maeve."

I smile. "Dean and I worked together to give it our own twist."

"It's been a few months since he left now. Do you miss him?"

"Yes, I miss him, especially when I need someone to lift heavy things or reach high shelves. Speaking of, I have to go find a ladder to get these tassels hung up." I gesture to the shiny decorations on the top of my box.

"He's not the only tall guy around, you know. I can give you a hand."

"Oh, I'm fine," I say. I've gotten used to going it alone. "I'm sure the hotel staff will have one handy."

Sam laughs, low and hearty. "They looked a little busy when I walked past. And what kind of friend would I be if I didn't step in to help?"

I glance behind me at the booth. Once I get these tassels up, the rest of the work is pretty much done, but the clock is ticking toward opening time. "I do need to get changed. Would you be willing to hang this up while I run to the loo?"

Sam frowns. "Wait a minute. You're not going to wear those fine leggings?"

He's looking at my legs?

I like that. I like that he's looking *a lot.*

"Sadly, no. I need to look like a professional. Ergo, no yoga pants."

Sam sighs. "Such a shame. But I guess I'll help you anyway."

I laugh and grab my bag of clothes. A rush of heat runs down the back of my neck at feeling Sam's eyes on me.

I tell myself not to read too much into Sam and his flirtations and head for the restroom, where I check that my makeup and blow-out have survived, then swap gym clothes for the red dress I picked for the occasion. It's the kind of dress that can go from the office to drinks at, say, a bar like The Magpie. The classic red color and not-quite-mini length are eye-catching, but I still look like a woman who owns a business.

I slip on my heels and head back to the booth. My mouth falls open when I see that Sam not only has finished hanging the tassels but also has set out my flyers for The Magpie.

"Sam, you are an angel," I gush.

"It was no trouble," he says, and when he turns around, his eyes take an obvious detour up my body.

The look he gives me is far from *angelic*.

It's fiery. Flirty. And a little bit dirty.

That heat zips right back up my neck again. Sam does something to me. Something I didn't entirely expect from someone who's been off-limits, and who kind of still is, thanks to his recent divorce.

"With that dress, I don't know that I'll be able to pay attention to my booth," he says.

"Please. It'll be easy. You'll have so many ladies flocking to you," I say, trying to cover this unexpected rush of *feelings* running riot in my body.

Sam's eyes twinkle with laughter. "Do they flock to me? I hadn't noticed."

I laugh. "Oh no, you're not trapping me into admitting that."

It *is* true though. At events or

out socially, Sam's always been a magnet for women. But he always had eyes exclusively for his ex. Does he still feel that way?

"Either way, good luck today," Sam says. "I'm sure you'll clean up."

"You too," I say, and then I turn to prep a few drinks, ready for the doors to open.

Still, it's hard to tear my eyes away from the handsome man as he walks to his booth beside mine.

Uh-oh.

I know this feeling.

This feeling can only lead to trouble.

It's the same feeling that led me to think that Jeremy was a good guy. A gentleman. Someone who would never hurt me.

In other words, the kind of feeling that lies.

If anything, liking Sam would be even riskier than dating a random man. The inevitable crash and burn would hurt more because he wouldn't be some random guy. I would lose a friend.

So, I need to pull it together and ignore the remnants of heat skating along the back of my neck.

Even though it feels so good.

3

MAEVE

By the time the event's over, I've made more small talk than I ever thought possible—which, as an experienced bartender, is saying something—and have run out of ways to describe The Magpie's "modern, inventive energy." I've also served hundreds of old-fashioneds, and I'm sure I smell like orange and whiskey.

I'm packing up the glassware and the decorations when Sam stops by, drumming his fingers on the booth.

"So, what's the report?" he asks.

I grin. "Got the word out, that's for sure. You?"

"I think I've got some people interested," he says. "We'll see if it translates to foot traffic. At the very least, I think there's a guy from the *City Times* who's going to do a piece on Sticks and Stones."

"Love that paper. That's great."

Sam shrugs, but I can tell he's excited. "They liked what I told them about the pool competitions I've been running. So we'll see."

He glances around my booth and then, without a word, starts taking down my higher decorations. I can't help but smile.

"Thanks," I say, setting a hand briefly on his shoulder. His strong, firm shoulder. "Dean used to help me with stuff like that. Too bad the prat had to go and fall in love."

Sam laughs. "From what I hear, someone did push him along the way."

I shrug, grabbing some of the flyers and tucking them in a box. "Who am I to stand in the way of true love?"

"You really knew right away that they'd be good for each other?"

Did I? I'd sensed that Fitz was Dean's type, and Dean had needed someone to shake up his life and get him out of the bar. And that spark between them?

Undeniable.

So I'd made sure he and Fitz reconnected the night after Fitz strolled into the bar.

I grin, nodding. "With those two? Absolutely. Or at least I knew they had incredibly hot chemistry."

"And that translates to love?"

"I think you could argue that true love needs true chemistry."

"Now you're philosophizing, Maeve."

"It needs more than that, obviously," I say. "You need trust and commitment and honesty. But to get off the ground, maybe, love needs chemistry. You need to be with someone who gets you."

Someone like you.

I push the thought away. Just because we share the same job doesn't make Sam right for me.

"Sounds like you're speaking from experience," Sam says thoughtfully.

"Maybe," I reply. "Only because it feels like everyone I know is falling in love these days."

"Tell me about it," Sam says in a beleaguered voice. "I've got my friend Tom's engagement party to go to next weekend. I already know I'm going to have to field tons of 'Where's Emily?' questions from people who don't know about the divorce."

"Yikes," I say, but I study his face, tracking it to see if there are any hidden traces of pain there. "That's gotta be rough."

"It is what it is. People will talk." He runs a hand along his jaw. "The thing is, Emily and I may have only formally split a few months ago, but we'd grown apart long before that. It was a mutual decision."

A little spark of something flickers inside me. Sounds like he's definitely moved on.

"But that doesn't mean I want to talk about it with every Tom, Dick, and Harry at this party. And God forbid I should show up with a date. Then I'm the jackass who moved on too fast, you know?"

Now we're not just dancing

near the topic of broken hearts.
We've landed on it.

"So . . . have you dated?" I
ask. "Since . . ."

He shrugs. "I sort of took a
break. I'm in no hurry to go
through all that again."

"I know what you mean," I
say. And because I do understand, and because he's a friend,
it only seems right to offer to
help.

A friend.

He is just a friend, I remind
myself.

"Would it help to go to the
party with someone you're just
mates with?" I ask.

Sam tilts his head, intrigued.
"Are you offering your services?"

"That makes it sound so
improper," I say.

"Sometimes improper is a
very good thing."

"Indeed it is," I add.

"But proper or improper, it

would be nice to go with a friend. Especially a friend who's a certified master small-talker."

"You know that just comes with the territory."

"I still wouldn't take it for granted. And, of course, I could return the favor at any time. Proper or improper. Unless you have someone else up to the task?"

I resist the urge to lament just how single I am.

But I do like the idea of going with him. Plus, I could use the return favor.

"I do have a charity event I have to go to in a few weeks," I say. "Dean always went with me, but since he's gone, it'd be great to have a friend there."

"I'd be happy to volunteer my services."

"All the proper and improper ones?" I ask, a little flirty.

Fine, *a lot* flirty.

"We'll start with proper, and a proper kiss." He takes my hand and brushes a kiss over my knuckle in a Victorian-style kiss. Tingles buzz from the connection, spiraling through my body in a rush. "I am ridiculously ready to be your partner in obligatory-event crime. For two dates with you."

That's all it is—just two pretend dates.

And as we say goodbye, I try to tamp those tiny tingles that felt nothing like *pretend*. They were all too real.

* * *

I text Sierra that night and tell her about the event and Sam, and she responds with a series of fire emojis.

Maeve: It's just friendly stuff.

Sierra: As if I believe that.

Maeve: You should believe it.

Sierra: As if you believe it!

Maeve: I swear I do.

Sierra: Of course you do. Wink, wink, wink.

In the time leading up to Sam's friend's engagement party, he and I start texting each other during the day at work. Mostly it's little jokes about our patrons. Sam takes our inside joke about bad drink orders and runs with it, sending me pictures of the worst drinks that people order at his bar. He also takes selfies of himself making exaggerated crying or gagging faces at the particularly terrible ones.

The notes give me a little dose of energy, and I love it. I love, too, that the tasting event worked to drive more traffic into The Magpie. And it turns out that Sam's bar isn't the only one to snag some media attention. We land write-ups in three different blogs, and one in particular calls us the "makers of the best old-fashioned in London."

I screenshot it and send it to Dean the moment it's live. He sends back the thumbs-up emoji.

Dean: Well deserved! You don't need me, Maeve.

I'm laughing when my phone buzzes again.

Dean: How's the flirty texting going with a certain fellow bar owner?

Maeve: I should never have told you about that.

Dean: And yet I'm so glad you did.

Maeve: Just friends, and you know it.

Dean: It's funny that you think I'd believe that. Maybe you've finally met your match.

Maeve: Don't you have a wedding to plan?

Dean: Just saying, it would save us a seat if Sam was your plus-one . . . Think about it.

Maeve: You are evil.

Dean: As best mates are.

* * *

On the day of the engagement party, Sam texts that he'll pick me up at my flat. Since it's a daytime party, I choose a fit-and-flare dress, light pink with a simple tulip pattern on the flared skirt, and I fashion my hair into a French twist.

When I open the door, Sam's eyes slowly widen. He swallows a little roughly and clears his throat. "Wow. You look . . . stunning."

Stunning doesn't sound just-friendly, but I like it. "It's not that fancy. I'm just trying to help you make a good impression."

"Oh, you've definitely made one," he says, and oh my, did he just go there?

I don't mind that he did.

But I'm also not entirely sure

if we *should* be playing these flirty games, so I gesture to his light-blue button-down. "We both look proper. You look nice too."

"I aim to please," he playfully responds, and we call a Lyft.

Inside the car, I ask about Tom, his recently engaged friend.

"We've become pretty good buds through our running group," he says as we swing past the park. "It's my relatively new hobby."

"New, as in, post-divorce?"

"Yes. Try not to be blown away by the coolness of it. But yup. I needed to do something to get out of the house. Turns out, Tom was doing it for the same reason—a little distraction after his last marriage ended."

I touch his hand, linger there, solely to offer him comfort.

For no other reason, of course.

"It sounds like you were trying to make the best of things," I say.

"I suppose that's a fair way of looking at it," Sam says, and he glances down at our hands, still touching, before looking up to meet my eyes once more. "Tom's a cool guy. His family is crazy rich, so the engagement party's going to be insane. I can't imagine what the wedding will be like."

I arch a brow. "He must love her a lot—to trust in love again after a divorce."

"He does." He shrugs, his eyes vulnerable. "Sometimes love doesn't work out. But then you get a second chance."

"This stuff's always hard, isn't it?" I ask, a little wistfully, as the car slows at a light. "Engagement parties and weddings.

After you've . . . gone through a breakup. They were hard for me right after my last one, anyway."

"When was that?" Sam asks softly.

"A while ago now. Jeremy was great . . . until I found out he was seeing someone on the side," I say, then shrug.

"He's a fool." Sam shakes his head. "What an idiot."

I shrug. "He was, but he also helped me realize what's important to me. I want a man I can trust. Someone who's easy to talk to."

Someone like you, I almost add, but hold myself back. Where did that thought even come from?

"But enough about me," I say, ready to change the topic. "Are you okay? With going to the engagement party today?"

For a moment, Sam stares out the window. I wonder if I've

gone too far, but then he smiles. "Yeah, I'm okay. I'm better since you're here."

He turns his palm up and laces our fingers together. The simple act sends shivers all up and down my body.

Alarm bells go off again, warning me to keep this friendly. But I don't entirely want to listen.

Especially as I drink him in. His sharp jawline. The way he runs his hands through his dark hair. The way his eyes light up when he talks.

The way he makes me feel safe.

Then, of course, there's the fact that his hand still lingers on mine.

He glances down at it and then at me. For a moment, all I can do is look into his eyes.

The eyes of a thoughtful, funny, *single* man.

The car pulls to a halt at Roehampton Club, jolting us out of the moment. Probably for the best.

We duck out of the car, and as Sam flashes me a grin, my stomach flips.

Deliciously.

And dangerously.

Warning me that I need to be cautious.

Because I've been burned, and I don't want to go through that again.

Roehampton Club is covered in beautiful greens with flower beds dotted throughout. A bar is set up on one end, and Sam and I head over to order drinks. On our way, a stunning woman with glossy blonde curls and a short white dress stops Sam to say hi.

"And who is this lovely lady with you?" the blonde asks with a knowing glance.

"This, Lily, is my good friend, Maeve," he says. "And, Maeve, this is Lily, Tom's fiancée."

"Congratulations. I'm so happy for you," I say, shaking her hand as she beams.

"Maeve's also in the bar industry," Sam says. "She owns The Magpie."

"I know that place. I was there a few weeks ago. Had the most delicious martini. The place was packed, but your bartenders were fast and polite," Lily says.

"That makes me very happy to hear," I say.

Sam beams. "The place is packed every night, and she runs it like it's nothing."

I blush, and as I'm about to talk up Sam's bar, a tall, broad-shouldered man comes over and gives Sam a big bear hug.

"This is Tom," Sam explains,

and Tom pulls me into an equally crushing hug.

"So glad you could make it," Tom says. "Make yourself at home. Enjoy the food." He stops to press a kiss to Lily's cheek and she smiles at him adoringly, clearly over-the-moon in love. "I need to steal this beautiful lady away. Lots of people to say hi to."

After they leave, Sam and I wander through the crowds, nibbling on the crab-stuffed mushrooms and spring rolls. He keeps me laughing with jokes and stories from his American childhood. We drink pinot grigio as he tells me about the major differences between Los Angeles and New York, saying that Los Angeles has better views, but New York has more honest people, and then saying London's a perfect mix of the two. We even talk about Dean and how we think he's fitting into American life.

"He's probably disgusted by parts of New York," Sam says. "All that greasy pizza."

I laugh. "You make him sound like such a stick-in-the-mud! He ran a bar. He's not afraid of grease."

"You don't know grease—not until you've had New York pizza."

"Maybe you'll have to show me sometime," I say.

Sam smiles. "Maybe I will."

Perhaps it's the wine, but that sensible part of me—pragmatic, smart Maeve—is quickly losing out to the Maeve who's been laughing all day with Sam. Before I can respond, the DJ starts up with toasts to the happy couple. Soon enough, he's calling everyone to the dance floor, and Sam stands and extends his hand to me.

"How about a dance?"

The prospect sends tingles down my spine, and it's the tingles that sound those warning bells again. Laughing is one thing. Shivers are another. Shivers leads to *more*, and *more* could lead to heartbreak.

Correction: tingles and shivers could lead to more, but they don't have to. I'm only agreeing to a dance. Nothing wrong with that. Hell, there's nothing wrong with any of this.

This is just a dance.

And *dance* is what we do.

Sam leads me to the floor by the hand, but there's a fast song playing, which is perfect. It's all fun and games and whirling and laughing. We get our groove on for two more songs before the DJ switches it up with a slower tune.

A couple's tune.

I sense more than see Sam's

questioning look. No pressure, just wondering. I'm not sure I'm ready for his arms around me, even in public.

So, I fan my face and say, "I'm parched. Ready for a break?"

He nods, not seeming to think anything of it. "I'll get us drinks. Meet you at the table?"

"I'm just going to nip over to the ladies' first."

While I'm there, I eye my flushed face in the mirror. *Get a grip, Maeve.* I'm having fun, flirting with that sexy American man. Why balk at a slow dance? People dance at parties.

I feel safe with him. No pressure. So, the question isn't so much can I trust him, but can I trust myself?

Back at the table, Sam has snagged us some cake along with our drinks. Later, he takes me home, and he's quite proper as he wishes me goodnight.

A blip—more than a blip—of disappointment surprises me. I wouldn't have minded an improper goodbye.

4

MAEVE

A few days after the engagement party, a bouquet of flowers arrives for me at The Magpie.

I eye them curiously, and the note too.

Maeve,
Thank you for suffering through
that with me. It might be the most
fun I've ever had at a required
social gathering.
Yours, Sam

How did he know about the sunflowers? It's not as if I've broadcasted that they're my favorite. How could he know that they remind me of summer days and fresh starts?

I text Dean immediately. He's the only one I've told about my love of sunflowers—I gushed to him about getting them for the opening of The Magpie.

Maeve: Did you tell him?

Dean: Tell who what?

I bet I can imagine his face right now. Hell, I don't need to imagine it. I FaceTime him, and immediately, a satisfied-looking Dean shows up on my screen. Looks like he's at his new bar —The Pub.

"Maeve, I'm about to—"

I don't let him finish. "You told him, didn't you? About these?"

I flip the screen so he can see the sunflowers, and then I flip back to me. Dean dares to look innocent. Not just pretending-to-look-innocent either. Actually innocent.

"I honestly have no idea what you're talking about."

"Oh," I say. "Is that so?"

Dean eyes me closely. "Wait a minute. Are those from a guy? Are you dating?"

"No," I say. "Sam sent these. As a thank you for going to his friend's party."

Dean laughs. "So you *are* dating."

I roll my eyes. "Never mind. What're you up to?"

"I'm sorting some deliveries here. Want to see?"

"I do," I say, and he shows me around The Pub.

"It looks great." Truly it does, but I also love seeing him so happy.

But I still have my sunflower mystery to solve.

"And you didn't tell him about the flowers?"

"I swear I didn't. I don't have that much of a cupid in me. Plus, some men, you know, remember things about the people they like."

I hum, kind of doubtful, then say goodbye.

I pace around The Magpie.

Sam could have gotten lucky. They're a popular flower, after all. But most men will send roses. These flowers . . . they're bright, joyful. So much like Sam.

I get out my phone, snap a picture, and send it to him. Then I type out a quick text.

Maeve: Thank you for these. How'd you know they're my favorite?

Sam: Good! I was hoping that hadn't changed. You mentioned it a while back. Something about the way they make everything seem just a little lighter and new again, right?

The memory comes back to me all of a sudden. Sam, Naveen, Anya, Dean—all of us walking along the Thames last summer. We talked about our perfect Sunday, and I'd casually mentioned that every Sunday should start with fresh flowers.

Sunflowers, in particular.

For exactly the reason he'd said.

But that was almost a year

ago. How in the world had he remembered?

Sam: It always stuck with me. Now, I can't see a sunflower without thinking about you.

And that's the sweetest thing anyone's ever said to me.

Maeve: You have a great memory. Really, thank you. I don't know how I'll make it up to you after the charity event. Somehow I don't think it would be the same if I sent you sunflowers.

For a minute, the bouncing dots keep appearing and disappearing on my screen. Then, finally, a message pops up.

Sam: You could wear those yoga pants again.

I laugh.

Maeve: The yoga pants really do it for you, huh?
Sam: Or jeans. Or anything, actually. I'm not really particular. You look good in everything, Maeve.
Maeve: You do too.

I want to keep flirting. But I'm still so wary. What if we are better off as friends? What if flirting leads to dating and it changes the whole dynamic, not just between us but in our circle of friends?

What if we don't like dating as much as we like being friends? There's no reset button. Even if we don't crash and burn, things can never be precisely the same.

I don't keep him hanging on a typing bubble while I think about all this. In fact, I dwell on it for a day, and then two.

I talk to Sierra, ask her advice over FaceTime.

"Is it crazy to date a friend?"

She whistles, low and worried. "You might be asking the wrong person."

"And why is that?"

She sighs, a sound both frustrated and wistful. "There's this guy . . . he's my brother's good friend and teammate. And I might, just might, have it bad for him. And he's a friend of mine. So it's very complicated."

"So stay away? That's your verdict?"

She laughs. "I'm not sure I can. What about you?"

That's a very good question.

I'm not sure I can either when it comes to Sam.

I mull the issue over more while business runs, while Sam and I exchange texts not just about terrible drink orders but more, and while my day starts to feel incomplete if I don't have a string of messages in our text thread by evening.

I'm a busy woman. I run my own business, and it takes up a lot of my time. I don't have time for one-night stands, particularly with men who throw around sleazy pickup lines and eye-fuck my boobs.

But Sam's not a one-night stand. He's gorgeous. Sweet. Smart. Funny. Kind.

It's time to throw caution to

the wind, starting with the return favor "date" Sam and I have lined up. It will mean exposing myself—sharing with him a part of me not many other people see.

But it's worth it. *He's* worth it.

It's time to expose myself to trouble.

The day of the Night for Lost Stars benefit, I set out for St. James' Park. I need fresh air and flowers and my favorite bench in my favorite spot.

Rows of yellow and orange blooms mix with blue and white ones, the petals dancing gaily in the breeze. Their beauty makes it harder to be sad, which is why I came.

Across from the bench where I sit, a white pelican zooms

across the lake. Dad was the one who first brought me here, and he loved to point out the pelicans and tell me about how they've lived here for almost four hundred years. It was one of his favorite places, and now it's mine too.

I can do this tonight.

I can tell Sam.

I can *trust* Sam with this vulnerable piece of me.

I head home from the park and shower. I twist my hair up into a chignon and choose some chandelier earrings that brush my neck. After some consideration, I pick out a violet dress with a slit up the side. As I swipe on some lipstick, my phone buzzes with a familiar ringtone.

"Hey, Mum," I say. "How're you?"

"Are you still at home? I thought you'd be on your way already."

I laugh. "It's not for a few hours. Don't worry. I'll be there on time."

"Does it really start so late? Seems like it was earlier when I went with you."

I roll my eyes. "Same time, Mum."

"There's something I want you to bid on," she says.

"I'm guessing you've been trolling the website since they announced the items?"

"You make it sound like a bad thing," she says. "I'm just being strategic. Now, there's a guitar I want. Signed by Ed Sheeran."

"Mum, that'll go for thousands of pounds," I say. "Some hedge fund manager will snag it."

"Hope springs eternal. You never know," she says.

"I'm pretty sure hope won't nab us the guitar. But if it makes you happy, I'll bid."

"Just for fun. And fun is good, right?"

I smile. "Fun is definitely good."

We chat some more about events in the past, then I say goodbye and hang up, holding the phone to my chest and thinking about fun, about good times.

Thinking about letting Sam in on this part of my life.

I take in a breath just as my doorbell rings.

Sam's here.

The timing seems prophetic.

I pull on my heels and grab my clutch. On the way out, I glance at myself in the mirror. Tendrils of hair frame my face, and not even an eyelash is out of place.

I'm ready.

Sam meets me at the door looking insanely sexy in a fitted suit. He sees me and whistles.

"Damn," he says. "This is how you should dress all the time."

I laugh. "Likewise. I don't know if I've ever seen you in a suit."

"Get used to it," he says. "If I have to wear this to get you to wear that, then suits are my new wardrobe."

"You're impossible," I say.

"And endlessly entertaining."

Sam's Lyft is still waiting as we reach the sidewalk. He opens the back door for me, and we slide in.

"I'm glad you liked the sunflowers," he says earnestly, and as I thank him again, meeting his gaze, we share a moment, something unspoken passing between us. "Did they make things seem lighter for you?"

Tha-thunk. My heart beats double time. "They did. They do," I reply, speaking the truth.

Time stretches out between us. Energy crackles like a live wire, sparking and spinning, and his lips, my God, I want to kiss them.

The car brakes to a jerky stop in traffic. The moment passes, gone.

Sam clears his throat. "So, what's this event tonight about? What're we saving? Animals? Babies?"

I don't answer right away. I take a breath first, wishing there weren't another person here. Still, our driver hasn't so much as glanced back since we got in, so I shouldn't use him as an excuse.

Time for honesty.

"It's to support ALS research, actually," I say. Prickles of hurt spike the backs of my eyes, but I blink them away. It hurts—God, it'll always hurt—but maybe time has started to work its magic. "Which . . . my dad died from."

"Oh," Sam says, his deep brown eyes going soft and sincere. "Maeve, I'm so sorry. I didn't know."

"It's okay," I say. "It was seven years ago. But my mum and I used to always go to this together. And then, Dean used to go with me, but now . . ."

"Now I'm here," he says. "And I've already made a joke of it."

"No," I say. "I'm glad you're here. Honestly, I don't know that I've ever told someone about my dad without crying. And now, look. Mascara still firmly in place."

I laugh, and Sam laughs with me. I feel lighter about this than I ever expected.

"Well, then, let's go raise as much money as we can in your dad's honor," he says as we pull into the event, then step out of the car. "Can I bid on a boat? I've always wanted to bid on a boat."

Laughing, I shake my head. "Did that tasting event really change things that much for your bar?" I tease.

He grips my hand, stops me. We're on a crowded sidewalk, but all the people blur into nothing and it's only me and him, him and me. "It did, Maeve," he says in that deep voice I'm coming to know, to love. "It changed everything."

I swallow the lump in my throat. He can't be talking about just the bar. Can he?

I don't get a chance to press, to ask more, as soon, Sam's taking my hand and walking me into Novotel London West. We make our way to the event space, passing people who look like they're made of money.

We check out the auction items, browsing through signed

movie posters and football jerseys and, finally, a signed Ed Sheeran guitar. It's white and glittery with a gold signature on the front.

"I have to bid on this for my mum," I say.

Sam looks down at the bidding card. "One thousand pounds."

Woah. "I'll tell her it was too high."

"Come on," Sam says. "I'll split it with you. We have to go in on this."

I shoot him a skeptical glance. "Sam, do you even like Ed Sheeran?"

"Doesn't matter," he says, dead certain. "We're doing this."

"And if we win, how are we going to split a guitar in half?" I fold my arms across my chest, but I can't hide my grin.

"We'll have joint custody.

Half the time at my place, half the time at yours."

"Ridiculous," I say, but I'm laughing, and that feels good too.

"It'll give you a reason to visit," he says in a flirty tone, and I like the way that sounds. I like it a lot.

We're outbid for the guitar before we've gotten more than ten paces away, but I send Mum a photo showing the bid, and she texts back with a crying-with-laughter emoji and says she appreciates that I tried.

The night I'd been dreading passes like that—the dazzling auction offerings making me ooh and aah, Sam making me laugh. The dinner and drinks are delectable. The event is fun, and it's so nice to be able to support a cause I'm passionate about. I appreciated these things when I attended with

Dean, but I'm not sure I *enjoyed* myself.

As the night winds down, Sam and I call another car. We tumble in, laughing about every-thing and nothing at all. We pull up to my flat, and there's no question—I've never left that event feeling this light or this good.

Sam did that. Sam, who kept my spirits up during the event. Sam, who remembered the sunflowers. Sam, who's kind and funny and thoughtful.

He walks me up my steps and takes my hand like it's the most natural thing in the world, and it is. Being with him is easy.

"We'll have to do this again sometime," he says, his lips curving into a knowing grin. "You know, I've got this wedding to go to. Not sure if you'd be interested. It's transatlantic."

"You don't say?"

He laughs, and I decide it's time for fun. For chances.

For choices.

I nibble on my lip, meet his gaze, and go for it. "Are you asking me on a third date?"

"I am," he says, and his eyes darken. "Will you attend Dean's wedding with me? And not because I don't want to answer questions about my ex. But because I like spending time with you. You're incredible, Maeve."

"You're incredible too," I say, and his eyes flicker to my lips as he cups my cheeks, brushes a rough thumb over my jaw. He hovers there, an eternity but a whisper away, and desire, emotion, and need hurtle through my body until I just can't take it anymore.

"Kiss me," I demand.

He doesn't need a second invitation.

His lips crash against mine in an explosion of lust. The tingles from earlier become a hurricane of want, of lust, and soon we're kissing like we don't want to come up for air. Like all we need is each other.

We stumble back up to my flat, kicking off heels and shoes and losing ourselves together. I catch a glimpse of the table where the sunflowers have lasted remarkably long in their vase, and I smile, as sure as I ever have been about a decision in my life.

Especially when our clothes vanish in seconds and we fall onto my bed. He fits me so well, our bodies magnets for the other. I pull him close, seeking him, needing him.

And soon, we're tangled together, skin hot, breath coming fast. I'm under him, and we move like water, gasping and moaning together.

His hands caress me tenderly, his lips slide across my skin passionately, and he takes me deeply.

We fall over the edge together.

5

MAEVE

A week later, I sip tea on my balcony, breathing in the steam from my mug. Cars stream by and the Thames stretches past in the distance. Behind me, my suitcase leans packed and ready against the door.

In a few days, my best friend will be married.

I'd planned to go solo. Catch the flight to New York and do a fair amount of crying.

But now, I'll be watching all of Dean's dreams come true, and at the end of the night, I won't be dancing alone. I'll be dancing with Sam.

Sam. Rugged, incredible, delicious Sam.

Memories of the last few nights rush through my mind. And last night too. I shiver as I remember Sam's hands traveling up my arm, sliding my dress off. The feel of his mouth on mine.

Since the Night for Lost Stars event, we've been making up for wasted time. Now that I've had a taste, I can't get enough of Sam.

I close my eyes, replaying how he pressed me back against the wall, anchoring me with his arms.

But I can't linger on the memories. I have a plane to catch, and messages to answer, including one from my California friend.

Maeve: You asked if it's worth it. To date a friend.

Sierra: And the verdict?

Maeve: Yes. Yes it is.

I picture Sam and I smile. This friendship, this passion, this connection.

Maeve: I'm so glad we took the chance. I can't wait to hear what you do with yours.

Sierra: Ha. Me too. I can't wait either.

After I close the messages, I check the time. I finish my tea and wash up, not wanting to return to a mess. In a few hours, Sam and I will be on a plane to New York. We'll have seven hours to spend together. With anyone else, I might be worried about how to spend the time.

But with Sam, I know I'll be entertained, one way or another.

The bell to my flat rings, and within moments, Sam's at the door, dressed in casual jeans and a tight shirt.

"Hey, beautiful," he says, dropping his suitcase to the floor. His hands go straight to my waist, and I smile. "You wore my favorite yoga pants."

"I did. I wore them for you." I press my body against his, and one hand slides up my back, tangles in my hair, tugs a little. "It's going to be a long plane ride, Sam."

"Then we're going to have to make this damn quick."

Our lips collide, and then it's

a race to see who can undress the other faster.

I win.

* * *

We don't arrive early at the airport. I'm not sure I've ever cut anything so close in my life, but Sam's crooked grin makes me think that some things are worth bending rules of punctuality for.

He steps close to me and tucks a loose strand of hair behind my ear. "Ready to go watch Dean get married?"

I take a deep breath and nod. "Absolutely."

We work our way through security and the usual checkpoints and onto the jetway. Sam makes everything feel easy, chatting to the flight attendants, his charm putting everyone at ease, including me.

We buckle in, and without a word, he takes my hand and laces our fingers together.

"Now, I do need to come clean about something," he says.

I freeze.

Uh-oh.

Is this it?

The point where my perfect fantasy comes crashing down around me?

He takes a deep breath. "I'm sort of . . . nervous about takeoff."

It takes me a minute to understand what he's saying. "You're afraid of flying?"

"No," he says playfully. "I didn't say that. You're putting words in my mouth."

"Sorry. You're nervous about flying," I tease, but not unkindly. He's sharing this piece of himself with me—this vulnerability, and I like it. "Thank you for telling me."

He shrugs, but behind that cocky exterior, vulnerability flashes in his eyes.

I run my hand along his cheek, drawing him closer. "It seems to me like this is just a big excuse to hold on to me."

He winks. "You've figured me out. Also . . . I should add that it's helpful if I have a distraction."

"Oh? What kind of distraction?"

He shrugs innocently. "Maybe the kind that involves you telling me what you plan to do once we get to our hotel room."

"Are you sure you want me to spoil the surprise?"

He grins in a way that says yes, oh yes, he would like some spoilers please.

"I was thinking how much I'd enjoy being bent over the sink

and watching us in the mirror," I say.

"Dear God in heaven, may this flight take two minutes," Sam growls. Then he whispers in my ear, "Good thing we have this row to ourselves. Keep talking."

I laugh as the pilot's voice comes over the intercom, and the flight attendants begin their tutorial. The plane moves under us, getting ready for takeoff, and his eyes slide closed as I continue to whisper into his ear about my plans for the evening. We stay like that until the plane's in the air, gliding along.

"Sam," I say, once we reach cruising altitude. "Looks like I don't need to distract you anymore."

He glances out the window. "Excellent. Now I can work on distracting you."

It's a good thing no one's

sitting next to us. By the time Sam starts describing how I'll look in the mirror, I wish this plane would land right now.

Hours later, when we check into our hotel, we break the speed record undressing, falling into one another, and making each of our spoken fantasies a reality.

6

MAEVE

The next day, we linger in bed, spending as much of the morning as we can tangled up together. Later, we meet Dean and the rest of the wedding party over at The Pub for a joint bachelor party. It's been closed to the public for the event, so we'll have the whole bar to ourselves.

As soon as we walk in, Dean crushes me with an embrace that turns into a group hug as Fitz barrels over and Sam jumps in. There are toasts, and then there's plenty of liquor, but not too much, because tomorrow our guys are getting married.

At one point, Dean and I peel off from the group, and he gives me another hug.

"I'm so happy for you," I say, tears in my eyes.

"And I'm happy for you," he says. "Looks like I was right. You did find your match."

I don't have words for that. I look over his shoulder at Sam, who raises a glass.

And I smile at my best friend, happy for both of us.

* * *

The next day, after a beautiful ceremony, Sam holds my hand as we watch Dean and Fitz take their first dance in the middle of the Loeb Boathouse's dance floor. As they finish, Sam presses a kiss against my temple, and warmth thrills through me. How could I have ever thought to say no to this?

"There's something we still need to do," Sam says. "Since we're here."

I raise an eyebrow at him. "What's that?"

"New York pizza," he says. "I'm going to prove to you that the grease is real."

I laugh. "It can't possibly be as horrid as you say."

"It can be bad, I assure you."

"Maybe I like being bad," I whisper, and he runs his hand over my knee.

"I like that about you very much," he says softly in return, his eyes worshipping me, and I have no doubt that I'm the only woman he sees.

He's running his hand along my knee when the DJ changes the song to "Thinking Out Loud."

"Oh my God," I say. "This is the guitar!"

"What?" Sam says, and then he listens. "Is this Ed . . . what's-his-name? The guy with the guitar that we bid on?"

I nod and laugh harder. "The guitar we were robbed of."

"It's a sign," Sam says. He stands next to me and holds out his hand. "We didn't get a chance to slow dance before," he says with a smile. "How about we fix that?"

My hand slides into his, and we glide over to the dance floor. I catch sight of Dean and Fitz dancing too, and my heart gives a tiny flip.

Remember when we promised this wouldn't be us? I think. And, as if he can hear me, Dean glances my way. He smiles and shakes his head before turning back to Fitz, looking like a guy who can't believe his luck.

I laugh as Sam twirls me. He catches me, and we're closer than ever. I look up into his eyes and find his are gazing right into mine.

"So, what're we going to do now that we're out of parties and events to go to?" Sam asks.

I pretend to think about it. "Hmm, I guess we'll just have to keep having mind-blowing sex all the time."

"Oh man," he says. "Not sure I'll be able to make that work."

"No?"

"I'd have to make it official first. Officially date," he says. "And you'll have to meet my friends."

I laugh, and he catches my mouth in a kiss. It's a shiver that doesn't go away, spreading from where his lips touch mine.

This is more than three dates.

This, I could do for a long time. Maybe even . . . forever.

And maybe, just maybe, I will.

* * *

We have our fourth date later that week. We go crazy and fly to San Francisco, where I see more of my stateside friends at Sierra's bar in Hayes Valley. The Spotted Zebra is fabulous, all pink and black-and-white striped and it's so very her.

I crush her in a hug when I see her, and then introduce her to Sam.

"And this is my . . ."

He extends a hand. "I'm her boyfriend."

And the grin that spreads across my face can't be stopped.

"You're next," I whisper when I hug her back.

"We'll see. We will definitely see."

Oh yes we will.

* * *

Is Sierra next? Want to find out what happens in her love life? Then grab the friends-to-lovers, wedding date, pretend romance THE VIRGIN REPLAY, available everywhere!

Enjoy the first chapter!

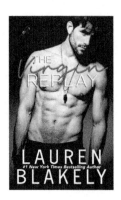

Sierra...

I'm pretty good at reading people—comes with being a bartender. But there's one customer I haven't been able to get a read on in the last year.

The guy who's putting the pool cues away in the game room at my bar.

At least, I can't get a read as to whether he'll ever ask me out.

Or ask me to go home with him.

With everyone else gone for the night and The Spotted Zebra already closed, I steal a moment to check out Chance Ashford as he lifts his multimillion-dollar right arm to place the sticks in the holder on the wall.

I'm enjoying the view of him *a lot*. Every time he comes by, I enjoy the view a little more. And then I wonder . . .

When he's done, the tall drink of a man turns around, wipes one palm across the other, and flashes me a winning grin. "That's done."

Best to keep things friendly, as they've always been, till I know where we might go from here. "Watch out. I just might enlist you in mopping and cleaning up," I say breezily.

His chocolate-brown eyes twinkle. "I just might say yes."

I laugh, then hook my thumb in the direction of the door. "Hit the road, Chance. You've got playoffs to rest up for."

Chance is the closing pitcher for the San Francisco Cougars, my second-favorite baseball team in the city. Since my brother became their starting catcher, the team has grown on me. Some of the guys on the team have become close friends over the last few years, stopping by my bar after games.

Like this man.

Chance is obviously far and away my favorite of the guys who stop by. He's easy to talk to and so damn easy on the eyes.

"I don't mind helping. Our first playoff game isn't for a couple days, so I don't have an early bedtime tonight. Besides, I'm still amped up from clinching."

I reach for a couple shot glasses left on the pool table. "But it's late, and star closers need their beauty sleep."

"That is true. Sleep is a beautiful thing. But I'll still help you finish up."

I can do it myself, but the team stayed late. The crowd was boisterous, and I won't turn down an extra pair of hands at this post-midnight hour.

And *those hands . . .*

As he gathers the beer bottles from the pool table, I study his long strong fingers and big palms that can wrap around a baseball. And perhaps a woman's hips.

Mmm, I like that image.

And what are you going to do about it, Sierra?

"Take these to the kitchen?"

I blink. Look up. Meet his eyes. A flush crawls up my chest as it takes me a few seconds to process his question.

"Yes, thanks," I say, my throat a little dry.

Good thing he didn't entirely catch me staring.

Chance takes the empties to the kitchen, places the bottles in the recycling, then sets the glasses in the sink. As we make quick work of washing and drying, I do my best to reroute my thoughts.

I can't keep crushing on him like this.

Or is it lusting?

Probably a little of both.

Chance finishes setting the chairs on the tables, and I decide that tonight, it's a crush. When I'm ready to say goodnight to The Spotted Zebra, I grab my purse from behind the counter and head for the door.

He holds it open for me.

"Thanks again. I appreciate it. You didn't have to stay behind," I say as I lock up the bar.

"I know I didn't have to. I wanted to," he says, his sexy voice a delicious rumble.

The crushy, lusty feeling definitely includes affection too. How can I help it when Chance looks at me with such genuine kindness, like it truly was his pleasure to help me out?

Kindness in a man I lust after? That would be potent.

He glances at his wrist even though he doesn't wear a watch. "It's late. Are you calling a Lyft or walking?"

I gesture in the direction of my apartment a few blocks away. "I don't live far. I'll walk."

He gives a crisp nod. "Then I'll walk you. And don't say I don't have to."

With a laugh, I gesture to the sidewalk. "I won't say that."

As we head down the block, we pass a group of fans decked out in Cougars gear, still a little rowdy from the team's victory, which secured them a Wild Card spot. A guy in glasses recognizes Chance, thrusts an arm in the air, and shouts, "Go, Cougs."

"Go, Cougs," Chance replies.

"So, I'm a little torn on something," I say once we turn on the next block.

"Yeah? What's that?"

"Who to root for in the playoffs."

He strokes his bearded jaw as if he's deep in thought. "Oh. Of course. That sounds like such a difficult dilemma."

I shrug. "It's not so easy. I've always been a Dragons woman."

He staggers, clasping a hand over his heart. "You did not just say that."

"I did," I say cheekily as we walk on. "More to the point, haven't you noticed my brother and I love to bicker about team versus family loyalty?"

Chance shakes his head in disbelief. "Grant is my catcher. How can you *not* be a Cougars fan? I assumed you were simply giving your sibling some sass."

"You know what they say about making assumptions," I tease.

He shakes a finger at me.

"That's a reasonable expectation, woman."

"Maybe it is. But one should always ask."

"Fine. You have me there. So, I'll ask now—why are you breaking my heart, Sierra?"

"I grew up a Dragons fan. I loved them when I was younger and old habits die hard," I admit with a shrug.

"Tell me, then, what's it going to take to fully convert you to the good side? Even the World Series victory last year wasn't enough?" His diamond-studded ring glints in the light from the streetlamps along my block.

I flash back to that glorious game—and the night I started having dirty dreams about Chance. I was at the ballpark for the game, and I'd hugged him after the win. His divorce had just been finalized and he was fully single, so maybe that's why

I started thinking about him in all new ways after one celebratory embrace.

"Fine," I say. "Winning it all last year did help a smidge."

We stop in front of my place. "Then, Sierra, I will just have to keep trying to convince you."

His eyes flicker with mischief.

Perhaps, dirty mischief?

Ohhh. I hope that's a yes. That my people-reading skills are on the ball right now.

Because even in the dark, I'm pretty sure I can read heat in his eyes—speculation in the way they travel up and down my body. The man wants me to ask him up.

And holy hell.

I want to invite him in.

No more noodling over possibilities, no more wondering.

I like the way he looks at me

—*a lot.* His hot gaze sends a zing down my body.

We're on the brink of something. A crossroads in our friendship where maybe we both want it to go to the next level.

Only, I want to be absolutely positive.

Don't want to make a mistake. To misread a man again.

I'm the opposite of impulsive. I plan my outfits down to my panties. I schedule my days and the drinks I'll make at night. And I definitely don't jump into bed with men.

Even though, I'm pretty sure I finally know where I want all this attraction with Chance to go. I can see the destination and I want to savor the journey. Each fun, flirty step to the bedroom for the very first time.

"Yes, you should keep trying," I say, officially flirting.

"Then I will," he says, giving it right back.

I wiggle my fingers in good-bye. "Good night, Chance. Good luck in the playoffs. Maybe I'll root for you."

He hums, tossing me a crooked grin. "Maybe I'll stop by The Spotted Zebra again."

"Ah, now you're being convincing."

"That's exactly what I want to be," he says.

And his arms are exactly what I want to feel around me.

So, I slide in for a quick hug, enjoying his warmth, the woodsy clean scent of him. I linger for a little longer and, oh yes, he does too.

When he ends the hug, he gestures to where my blonde hair curls over my shoulder. "By the way, nice pink streak. Glad you changed it from Dragons purple."

Reflexively, I lift a hand, smoothing the splash of color.

"But pink isn't the Cougars color," I point out.

"But it's not the Dragons color anymore either. So, I'll take it as a sign to keep up my *Be a Cougars Fan* campaign," he says with a grin.

"Keep campaigning, Chance."

"Count on it," he says, his voice a little husky.

"And thank you for walking me home. You're a good guy," I say as I push open the door to my building.

"And I'm a convincing one," he says.

And as of tonight, I think he could be a promising one.

It's a late September evening, and with the way his eyes sparkled in the night, I'm pretty sure I know who I want to be my first.

The man walking away from me.

THE VIRGIN REPLAY is available everywhere!

ALSO BY LAUREN BLAKELY

FULL PACKAGE, the #1 New York
Times Bestselling romantic
comedy!

BIG ROCK, the hit New York
Times Bestselling standalone
romantic comedy!

THE SEXY ONE, a New York
Times Bestselling standalone
romance!

THE KNOCKED UP PLAN, a
multi-week USA Today and
Amazon Charts Bestselling
standalone romance!

MOST VALUABLE PLAYBOY, a
sexy multi-week USA Today
Bestselling sports romance! And its
companion sports romance, MOST
LIKELY TO SCORE!

WANDERLUST, a USA Today

Bestselling contemporary romance!

COME AS YOU ARE, a Wall Street Journal and multi-week USA Today Bestselling contemporary romance!

PART-TIME LOVER, a multi-week USA Today Bestselling contemporary romance!

UNBREAK MY HEART, an emotional second chance USA Today Bestselling contemporary romance!

BEST LAID PLANS, a sexy friends-to-lovers USA Today Bestselling romance!

The Heartbreakers! The USA Today and WSJ Bestselling rock star series of standalone!

P.S. IT'S ALWAYS BEEN YOU, a sweeping, second chance romance!

MY ONE WEEK HUSBAND, a sexy standalone romance!

CONTACT

I love hearing from readers! You can find me on Twitter at LaurenBlakely3, Instagram at LaurenBlakelyBooks, Facebook at LaurenBlakelyBooks, or online at LaurenBlakely.com. You can also email me at laurenblakelybooks@gmail.com

Printed in Great Britain
by Amazon